Planet Kayterus

The Flying Orange

A Black Hole

The Space Giant's Beanstalk

Oddball

Major Tom

Series 814

The Fun Guys Stories:

The Adventures of Major Tom:

First edition

© LADYBIRD BOOKS LTD MCMLXXXIV

Adventures of Major Tom

Space Invasion Skyhawk

written and illustrated by PETER LONGDEN

Ladybird Books Loughborough

Major Tom and Oddball were cruising through the galaxy, on space patrol in the Flying Orange, when they received an urgent message from base control. "Switch on the televiewer, Oddball," ordered Tom.

Pictures from the planet Midas were beamed up to the Flying Orange. They showed Skyhawk the Mighty and his evil army of Hawkdroids. They had invaded the peace-loving planet and were looting the cities. "This is just the beginning," said Tom. "Skyhawk intends to raid every planet in the galaxy. It's up to us to stop him!"

"I'll check with Alphonse to see where Skyhawk's hideout is," said Oddball.

Alphonse the computer reeled out the answer. "SKYHAWK THE MIGHTY...HOME BASE IS A PLANET ON THE FAR SIDE OF THE RED NEBULA...APPROACH WITH CARE."

7

"Set a course for the star system – Red Nebula, Oddball," commanded Tom.

Oddball plotted the route and soon the Flying Orange was hurtling through space on hyper-speed. The two heroes had no time to lose if they were to stop this villain!

"Skyhawk's planet straight ahead, sir,"
shouted Oddball, as he put the orange
back into cruise speed. The Flying
Orange passed through the outer rings
of the planet and Major Tom peered
through the telescanner for a landing
place.

Suddenly the orange's warning system flashed. "What is it, Oddball?" gasped Tom.

"Large unidentified flying object, closing in on us at great speed," came the reply.

"Switch on the visual monitor," said Tom.

The monitor showed a huge spacecraft coming towards the Flying Orange.

"It must be Skyhawk's spaceship. We'll never outrun it!" cried Oddball.

13

Huge metal claws opened up and grabbed the Flying Orange in mid air. But unseen by the attacking ship, Tom and Oddball had escaped in Segment One. The high speed mini ship peeled away from the orange before the talons closed tight.

''We may have lost the Flying Orange for the time being, but at least we'll be led to Skyhawk's headquarters!'' chuckled Tom.

Major Tom and Oddball followed the Hawkplane at a safe distance and watched as it landed on what looked like a huge nest, on the top of a volcano.

"What an amazing hideout," said Tom, as they circled the volcano. It was completely surrounded by water and swampland.

"The only entrance seems to be through that nest," observed Oddball.

Segment One landed in the swampland.

"Wait here, Oddball, while I take a look around," said Tom.

The Major climbed on to a large rock to take a better look. But the rock moved and then began to growl. Tom leapt off as he realised what he'd been standing on. It was a sabre-tooth swamp rock, a deadly eight-legged monster, and it lunged forward snapping its teeth. Tom just managed to scramble away and went deeper into the swamp.

Carefully, Major Tom made his way through the rotting weeds, until he stopped suddenly. He had run straight into a Hawkdroid patrol.

''Freeze! Move and we'll fire!'' shouted one of the robots, in a tinny voice.

The other robots now turned their guns on Tom and marched him off to the volcano.

The Hawkdroids stopped at the base of the volcano and a hidden entrance began to open.

"Inside, cat!" hissed one of them.

Major Tom was taken straight to Skyhawk the Mighty.

"We have captured the intruder. What are your instructions, mighty leader?"

"Who are you?" snapped Skyhawk.

"I'm the famous Major Tom and I'm here to arrest you!" said Tom.

Skyhawk the Mighty roared with laughter. "Come with me!" he bellowed. "See what you feeble earthlings are up against."

Skyhawk led Major Tom to the control room – the centre of his headquarters.

"From here, in my computer centre, I can control my army of Hawkdroids. They are indestructible. Soon I will have a thousand more Hawkdroids, all programmed to obey me."

"We need to destroy this control room," thought Tom but his thoughts were soon interrupted by the awful scream of Skyhawk. "Take him to the sea chains. Nobody lives to tell my secrets!"

Two Hawkdroids took Tom deep down into the base of the volcano. Another entrance opened and Tom was forced out onto a platform. Two chains were fastened to the outer wall. These were strapped to Tom's wrists. The Hawkdroids laughed as one of them explained what would happen.

"When high tide comes you will be completely covered with sea water."

"You metal monsters!" seethed Tom. "I'm not finished yet!"

"You soon will be!" they scoffed, as they wheeled away.

The water was soon gushing around Major Tom's legs as he struggled to free himself from the chains.

Tom stopped. He'd heard something. It was Segment One. In all the excitement Tom had forgotten about Oddball.

The little robot had been circling the volcano searching for him. He reached the Major just in time. The water was rising fast.

Oddball unstrapped a laser gun and took careful aim – ZAP! Two shots rang out and the chains were snapped in half.

"Well done, Oddball," shouted Tom.

"We'll saw off these shackles and then we must plan Skyhawk's downfall. They have no idea about you and they believe I'm drowning!"

''In that case we have the upper hand, sir,'' exclaimed Oddball. ''We can surprise them!''

Tom swam over to Segment One.

Later, with the shackles removed from his wrists, Major Tom and Oddball set off for the volcano.

"Bring the laser gun, Oddball."

Oddball and Tom used the stepping stones to cross the swamp. They soon found the hidden entrance and, as it opened, the two crimefighters stepped inside.

"This way," whispered Tom.

Tom and Oddball could hear a great deal of banging and the sound of moving machinery. They peeped over a balcony.

"We're on the production level," said Tom. Specialised Hawkdroid workers were busily building hundreds more Hawkdroids for Skyhawk's army.

"Unless we smash the control room, the Universe will be over-run with them," sighed Tom. "If I can draw their attention, Oddball, you can slip into the control room and blow up the main computer with the laser gun."

Tom sneaked down the passage but he tripped over and went sprawling at the feet of two guards.

"It's that cat," yelled one of the Hawkdroids.

"Let's take him to Skyhawk," said the other. The captured Tom was led away once more...!

"Well done, Major," thought Oddball.

"How brave to pretend to fall."

Oddball rushed into the control room.

Oddball quickly worked out which was the main computer. Then he took aim and fired.

There was a huge explosion and one by one each of the complex machines blew up in a storm of sparks and smoke.

''Within minutes the control room will be destroyed for ever,'' smiled Oddball. ''The power of the Hawkdroids will be gone.''

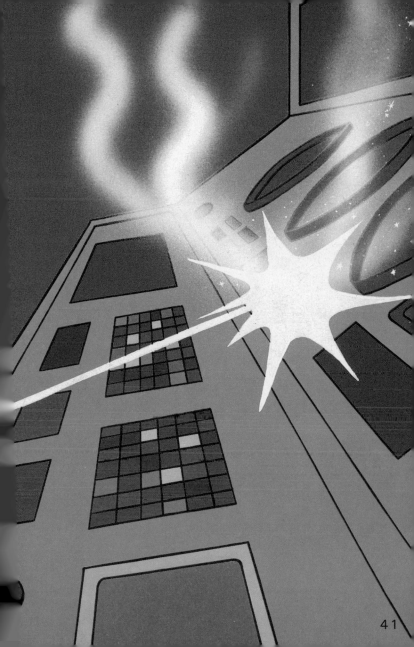

Meanwhile, Tom was back face to face with Skyhawk.

"I don't know how you escaped, but it will do you no good," he raged. "Hawkdroids, finish him off!!!"

But the order came too late, for the Hawkdroids started to spark and smoke poured from their control boxes.

"Oddball did it!" yelled Tom. "Your Hawkdroids are now useless; your computer complex is destroyed. You're *finished*, Skyhawk!!!"

SS Moon Cheese

Pisces

Little Bear

A Magnetic Field

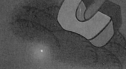

Great Bear